P9-CBP-475
BY
TOMIE DE PAOLA
ANDY
(THAT'S MY NAME)
ALADDIN PAPERBACKS

First Aladdin Paperbacks edition August 1999 Copyright © 1973 by Tomie dePaola
Aladdin Paperbacks An imprint of Simon & Schuster Children's Publishing Division
1230 Avenue of the Americas, New York, NY 10020
All rights reserved, including the right of reproduction in whole or in part in any form.
Printed and bound in the United States of America
10 9 8 7 6 5 4

The Library of Congress has cataloged the hardcover edition as follows:
dePaola, Thomas Anthony. Andy: that's my name.
Summary: Andy's friends construct different words from his name: "an" words, "and" words, and "andy" words.
I. Title. PZ7.D439An [E] 73-4593
ISBN 0-671-66464-6 ISBN 0-689-82697-4 (Aladdin pbk.)

WELL,
WHAT DO WE DO NOW?

ANDY

CAN I PLAY?
NO!
YOU'RE TOO LITTLE!

HEY GANG!
LOOK!
THAT'S
MY NAME..
ANDY

HERE KID!

OKAY! EVERY BODY MAKE A WORD!

FAN
MAN

PAN
RAN

TAN

CAN I HAVE MY NAME BACK NOW?
NO!

PUT THIS AT THE END.
HEY!

MY TURN.
HAND
B

BAND

B
SAND

T
SAND

STAND

DA-DAH!
LAND

GIVE ME THAT!

HANDY

DANDY
HANDY

SANDY
DANDY

CANDY
SANDY
DANDY

OOOF
BOO!

WAIT JUST A MINUTE!

YOU WON'T LET ME PLAY, SO I'M GOING TO TAKE MY NAME AND GO HOME!

ANDY
I MAY BE LITTLE, BUT....... I'M VERY IMPORTANT!

ANDY